Billy on the Ball

First published 2005
Evans Brothers Limited
2A Portman Mansions
Chiltern Street
London W1U 6NR

British Library Cataloguing in Publication Data

Harrison, Paul
        Billy on the ball. – (Twisters)
        1. Children's stories – Pictorial works
        I. Title
        823.9'2 [J]

ISBN 0237529262
13-digit ISBN (from 1 January 2007) 9780237529260

Printed in China by WKT Company Limited

Series Editor: Nick Turpin
Design: Robert Walster
Production: Jenny Mulvanny
Series Consultant: Gill Matthews

Billy on the Ball

Paul Harrison
and Silvia Raga

It's cup final day.

Billy's on the team.

The ground is full.

9

The game kicks off.

Billy heads the ball...

...and gets fouled.

Yellow card!

Billy's on the ball again.

He shoots,

he scores!

He's won the game!

He gets the trophy.

He lifts it high.

He wakes up!

Why not try reading another Twisters book?